For my mother, Madeleine Grandbois, who told me
many beautiful stories, including this one
—M. de V.

To once-little Molly Hanessian for being an inspiration
—L. G.

A NOTE ABOUT THE TEXT

In the part of Canada where this story is set,
French is the official language. That is why Matine
calls her mother "Maman" and her father "Papa."

Atheneum Books for Young Readers

An imprint of Simon & Schuster Children's Publishing Division

1230 Avenue of the Americas, New York, New York 10020

Text copyright © 2004 by Monique de Varennes

Illustrations copyright © 2004 by Leonid Gore

All rights reserved, including the right of reproduction in whole

or in part in any form.

Book design by Ann Bobco

The text for this book is set in Golden Cockerel.

The illustrations for this book are rendered in acrylic and

pastel on paper.

Manufactured in China

First Edition

10 9 8 7 6 5 4 3 2 1

Library of Congress Cataloging-in-Publication Data

Varennes, Monique de.

The sugar child / Monique de Varennes ;

illustrated by Leonid Gore.

p. cm.

"An Anne Schwartz Book."

Summary: When a child made of marzipan candy mysteriously

comes to life, her loving parents and friends shelter and protect her,

but there comes a time when she must risk herself for a friend.

ISBN 0-689-85244-4

[1. Fairy tales. 2. Friendship—Fiction. 3. Sick—Fiction.]

I. Gore, Leonid, ill. II. Title.

PZ8.V256Su 2003

[E]—dc21

2003000314

THE SUGAR CHILD

WRITTEN BY MONIQUE DE VARENNES

ILLUSTRATED BY LEONID GORE

AN ANNE SCHWARTZ BOOK
Atheneum Books for Young Readers

NEW YORK LONDON TORONTO SYDNEY

In a village tucked deep in the mountains of Canada there lived two bakers, Thérèse and Jacques. They loved their work, and they often sang as they spun flour and sugar into tasty little cakes. All year long their shop smelled as sweet as Christmas.

Each day, along with their loaves and pastries, Thérèse and Jacques baked a tray of little cakes to give away to the children of the village. They welcomed the little ones' shining eyes and bright faces, for there was one thing missing from their lives: They had no child of their own.

Every now and then Jacques made marzipan candy as a special treat. It tasted like sweet almonds and could be colored and shaped to look like almost anything: owls or oranges, boats or beavers, cherries or china dolls. The children thought it was wonderful, like having a toy they could play with and eat, too.

Late one spring night, as Jacques worked on a batch of marzipan, he began to think of the child he'd never had. Idly his hands shaped the dough into his dream child. Her hair was black and curly, her expression sweet; she seemed ready to break into a smile. She was slim—he was a little short of marzipan—but well formed. Her dress was a bright, bright red.

When he was finished, Jacques stared in wonder at the beautiful girl he had created. It was as if his longing had stolen into his fingers and made him an artist for just this one night. He smiled to think how surprised Thérèse would be when she found this lovely sugar child in the morning. And taking his candle with him, he went off to bed.

A few hours later he awoke to Therèse's cries. "Jacques, get up!

There's a strange girl sleeping in the kitchen!"

Jacques sat up groggily. "That's not a real girl," he laughed. "I made her out of marzipan." "Well," Thérèse answered, "it must be a strange batch of candy, indeed, for your marzipan girl just rolled over in her sleep!"

Jacques bolted for the kitchen. There on his pastry board lay a little girl! As he watched in amazement, she stretched and opened her eyes.

"Papa, Maman," she called out sweetly, "I have just had the most delicious sleep!" And she held out her arms to Thérèse and Jacques.

The first villagers to come to the shop that morning found the bread unbaked and the happy couple celebrating the arrival of their new daughter. In no time everyone in the village had heard the wonderful news. Thérèse and Jacques named their child Matine, from the French word for morning, for that was when she had come into their lives.

She was all they had ever wanted.

Matine was not, however, exactly like other children. Her skin was cool and a bit hard, like a fine sugar crust, and so thin you could nearly see through it. Jacques and Thérèse knew that although Matine spoke and played like a child, she was still made of a kind of fairy candy, and they feared that one day she would disappear as quickly as she had come. Hot sun could melt her, or rain. But Matine's own salt tears could melt her fastest of all.

At first the two bakers kept their daughter close. But soon they saw that she longed to play with the other children, and fearing her tears, they let her go.

The boys and girls watched over her
tenderly, guiding her into the shade when the
sun grew hot and wrapping her in their own
hoods and scarves at the first drop of rain.
Perhaps because she was made of sugar,
Matine's nature was unusually sweet, and the
other children were never tempted to make
her cry.

Matine loved them all and smiled like
the sun when they came tapping at the
bakery window.

But one child, Jean-Paul, was her favorite.

Matine met him on her second day of school. It was raining, and she sat in the schoolroom, watching through the window as the others played outside.

To her surprise, a boy sat down beside her. His hair was as dark and curly as her own, and his eyes were the golden brown of maple syrup.

"You don't have to stay with me," she told him. "I don't mind being alone."

"When it rains, I have to stay inside too," he said with a gentle smile. "I get sick easily—they say my lungs are weak. We can keep each other company."

At first they felt shy,

but they soon became great friends . . .

and looked forward to their time together more than anything.

One morning, however, Jean-Paul was not in class. Matine asked the others where he was, but no one knew. After school she rushed home, hoping her parents could tell her.

"Papa, Maman, where is Jean-Paul?"

Her parents exchanged troubled looks. Then Jacques said, "Don't worry, Matine. He's visiting his uncle in Montreal."

"Will he be gone long?"

"Perhaps," said her father, hugging his daughter tight. "Don't cry, my dearest. You know you can't cry." And Matine blinked back the tears.

Now, the truth was that Jean-Paul was still in their own village. But he had fallen ill, so ill that no one knew if he would get well. Matine's parents did not dare tell her, for if she began to cry, she might melt away forever.

Every morning Matine looked eagerly for her friend in school, but Jean-Paul's seat remained empty. Every afternoon she asked her parents if he had written, but no letter came. Every day she forced herself yet again not to cry.

As for Jean-Paul, he had by now burned through the worst of his fever, yet still he did not get better. Summer came, and he lay in his bed, growing ever more thin and weak. *Where is Matine?* he wondered. *Why doesn't she come to see me?*

No one told Jean-Paul that Matine thought he was far, far away.

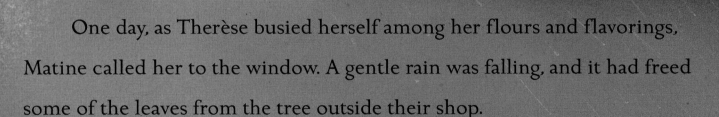

One day, as Therèse busied herself among her flours and flavorings, Matine called her to the window. A gentle rain was falling, and it had freed some of the leaves from the tree outside their shop.

"Look, Maman, those leaves are falling!" cried Matine, a little worried.

Therèse put her hand on her daughter's shoulder. "Yes, it's your first autumn. In the beginning a few leaves will fall, then many, until all the branches are bare. And bare they will stay until spring comes again."

Therèse sighed. "Seeing that tree reminds me of poor Jean-Paul." She stopped herself, but it was too late.

"Jean-Paul? Why 'poor Jean-Paul'?" Matine asked. Then she knew.

"He is ill, isn't he? He never did go away."

Thérèse had no choice but to tell her the truth.

"I must go see him at once!" Matine cried, throwing on her cloak.

"But it's raining!" Thérèse protested.

"Then I will cover myself up." Matine drew a hood over her head and rushed outside. She ran and ran, till at last she reached her friend's house.

There Matine found Jean-Paul lying white and still in his bed. His eyes were open, but he was so weak that he hardly recognized her. Matine could not help herself; she began to cry.

And it was just as her parents had feared. Each tear carved a tiny rivulet in the fragile surface of Matine's skin, melting it away. She bent over Jean-Paul, and one of her tears fell on each of his cheeks. At first a small red spot, like a bee sting, formed under the two glistening drops. Then the color spread and softened, until his cheeks glowed a healthy pink.

"Matine!" he exclaimed, with the shadow of a smile. "You came at last. And look, your skin is so pretty." He reached a weak hand toward her.

Surprised at his words, Matine gently touched her cheeks. Under the brittle layer of her marzipan skin was not more sugar, but the warm flesh of a real child.

Matine was filled with happiness. Without a word
she walked out into the rain and let the gentle drops wash
the last of the sugar away. She touched her skin again,
wondering at its softness. Then Matine danced with joy in
the warm rain, for she knew she was a real child at last.